This
Postman Pat Annual
belongs to

....

....

Postman pat ®

Annual 2008

Contents

Busy, Busy Greendale	8
New Arrivals	14
Postman Pat and the Greendale Knights	16
Pat's Picture Bingo	24
Postman Pat's Hedgehog Hideaway	26
Postman Pat's Noisy Day	32
Postman Pat the Hilltop Hero	36
Pat the Hero!	42
Postman Pat's Pet Rescue	44
Count with Postman Pat	50
Postman Pat and the Go-kart Race	52
The Greendale Go-kart Race Game	60
Postman Pat's Christmas Eve	62
Pat's Quiz	68

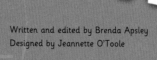

EGMONT
We bring stories to life

First published in Great Britain 2007 by Egmont UK Ltd
239 Kensington High Street, London W8 6SA

Written and edited by Brenda Apsley
Designed by Jeannette O'Toole

Stories adapted from original scripts by Colin Davis, Rachel Dawson, Davey Moore, Diane Redmond, Peter Reeves and Rebecca Stevens.

ISBN 978 1 4052 3172 5
10 9 8 7 6 5 4 3 2 1
Printed in Italy

Hello there!

Welcome to my new annual!
I hope you enjoy the stories and puzzles!
Read about when a new face
in Greendale rescued Jess,
when I had to do
something very scary –
and find out who won the
Greendale Go-kart Race!

Busy, Busy Greendale

Greendale is a busy little village. The people who live there are always out and about. There's always something going on!

Beep, beep!

Here comes **Pat Clifton** in his little red Post Office van. Pat's the village postman, and he uses his van to deliver the post every day. Everyone calls him Postman Pat.

PAT 1

Pat's "helper" always sits in the passenger seat of the van. It's his black and white cat, Jess. He goes everywhere with Pat!

Pat lives at Forge Cottage with his wife, **Sara**. She works at the Greendale Light Railway Station café and loves baking cakes for the people who come in for a snack.

Pat and Sara have a son, **Julian**. He's six years old and he's mad about football, just like his dad!

Every morning, Pat goes to the Post Office in the High Street to collect the post. **Mrs Goggins** works there.

Jess likes playing with Mrs Goggins' little white dog, **Bonnie**.

9

Postman Pat takes the post all over Greendale. Being a postman is the perfect job for a friendly person like him. He knows everyone – and everyone knows him!

Parp, parp! Here's **Doctor Sylvia Gilbertson** with her shiny white sports car. She makes sure everyone in Greendale is fit and healthy.

Doctor Gilbertson's daughter Sarah is eight, and she's a real chatterbox!

Reverend Peter Timms, the Greendale vicar, lives in a house next door to the church.

Neenaw, neenaw!

PC Arthur Selby is the Greendale policeman. He's always out and about in his blue and white police car.

His daughter **Lucy** is seven, and she just loves dressing-up.

Jeff Pringle is the Greendale Primary School teacher.

His son **Charlie** is seven and is a pupil at the school. He loves computers!

Postman Pat takes the post to farms and houses in the countryside around Greendale.

Chug, chug! Alf Thompson rides

around on his big red tractor. He and his wife **Dorothy** keep pigs, sheep, chickens, geese and goats on their farm. Their son **Bill** is nine and he has a pet sheep called Bessie.

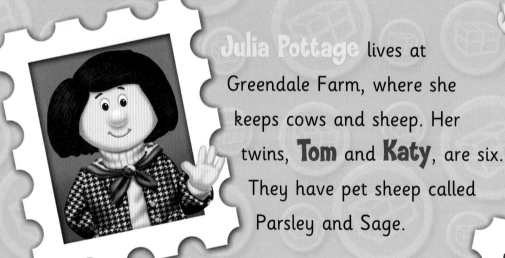

Julia Pottage lives at Greendale Farm, where she keeps cows and sheep. Her twins, **Tom** and **Katy**, are six. They have pet sheep called Parsley and Sage.

Honk, honk! Here's Ted Glen.

He drives a big lorry and lives at the Watermill. He's the Greendale handyman and can fix just about anything.

12

Pat likes taking post to the Greendale Light Railway Station. He can pop in to see Sara in the café.

Peep, peep! Here comes the Greendale Rocket! **Ajay Bains** drives the big green steam engine to and from Pencaster. He's the Station Master as well, so he's always busy!

Nisha, Ajay's wife, works at the railway as well. She sells tickets and serves in the café with Sara.

Ajay and Nisha's daughter is called **Meera**. She's seven and loves being big sister to her baby brother, **Nikhil**.

New Arrivals

Greendale is always changing. Some people move out to live in towns and cities. Some people move into the village to start new lives there.

Beep, beep!

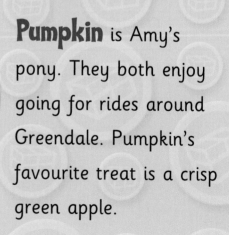

Here's Amy the vet, who has just moved to Greendale. She has opened a new animal clinic and drives around in her big green jeep. Read about how she helped Jess on page 44.

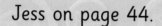

Pumpkin is Amy's pony. They both enjoy going for rides around Greendale. Pumpkin's favourite treat is a crisp green apple.

Colour in this picture of Amy and Pumpkin. Draw some more apples for Pumpkin.

Amy and **Pumpkin** by ....

Postman Pat and the Greendale Knights

One morning, Mrs Goggins had some parcels for Pat.

"They're plants," said Pat. "Sara's going out for the day, so I'm tidying up the garden as a surprise for her."

At Forge Cottage, Julian, Bill, Lucy and Meera were playing
a game of knights.

Julian knelt down. "I knight you **Sir Julian**, Knight of Greendale,"
said Bill, proudly.

"Can I be a knight?" asked Meera.

"No," said Bill. "Girls can't be knights."

"Oh, yeah?" said Meera.

"Yeah," said Bill. "They have to fight **dragons** and stuff. They have
to be strong."

When Pat got home, he took some
of the parcels out of his van.

Lucy wanted to help. She grabbed
a big parcel, but it was much too
heavy for her.

"I told you, girls can't be knights,"
said Bill. "You're not strong enough."

"Oh, yes we are!" said Meera.

She grabbed a parcel. Meera wanted
to show how strong she was.

So did Bill! But they both tripped and fell over!

"You'd better leave the parcels to me," said Pat.

"OK, Dad," said Julian. "Come on, we'll look for dragons!"

"D-d-d-dragons?" said Lucy.

Thud!

"See, girls are scared of everything," said Bill.

"Well I'm not!" said Meera.

Just then, Lucy heard a loud noise. It made her jump.

"It's a **d-d-dragon!**" she said.

"It's Dad's tractor," said Bill. "Only a girl would be scared of a tractor!"

Alf unloaded the arbour he had brought for Pat.

"You make it into an arch shape, plant roses round it, and they grow up the sides," Pat explained.

Then Pat dug a new flower bed. The empty compost bags gave him an idea! He cut neck and armholes in one, and put it on Julian.

"There you are," he said. "Armour!"

Pat made armour for the others. Then he made visors and shields from the plant boxes. Wooden spoons made good swords!

"Now we can fight like **real knights!**" said Julian.

"Take that!" said Meera.

"Take that!" said Bill.

Clank!

"Oh, please stop," said Lucy.
"I don't like fighting!"
Julian had no one to fight
with! "Maybe Bill's right," he
said. "Girls can't be knights."

Crrrassh!

Meera and Bill got a bit carried away! **"Look out!"** said Pat.
Too late! They crashed into the arbour and knocked it flat.

"I think that's enough fighting," said Pat. "Go and have a drink
to cool down."

There was a big surprise waiting for the Greendale knights when
they went back into the garden. Pat had made a castle out of the
plant boxes.

Bill, Meera and Julian went inside. They left Lucy outside to guard
the castle.

When Lucy saw smoke coming from behind the house she told the others.

"Is it a **dragon?**" asked Meera.

"No, it's a scary knight!" said Bill. "Look, he's got a **fire sword!**"

"**Hide!**" said Julian.

Poor Lucy was on her own. She wanted to hide, but she was on guard. "I have to protect the castle," she said. "I **must** be brave."

She picked up the water hose, turned it on, and fired it at the knight.

Splasshh!

But it wasn't a knight, it was Ted! He had come to fix the arbour with his blow torch! **Splash!** He was drenched!

The knights came out of the castle.

"You saved us, Lucy," said Julian.

"Yes, you were really brave," said Bill.

Julian asked Pat to knight Lucy. He touched her shoulders with a wooden spoon. "I knight you **Lady Lucy** Selby," he said.

The knights helped Pat to finish the garden.

When Sara came home she could hardly believe her eyes! "Oh, it's lovely," she said. "Thank you, Pat!"

"Don't thank me," said Pat. "Thank the **Greendale knights!**"

Pat's Picture Bingo

Play this fun game with Pat!

Look very carefully. Can you find these 10 little pictures in the big picture on the next page? Tick a box for each one you find. When you have found all 10 shout, **"Bingo!"**

24

"Bingo!"

Postman Pat's Hedgehog Hideaway

Sara was going away for the night. Pat and Julian went to the station to say goodbye.

"Bye!" said Sara. "Don't forget your packed lunch, Julian."

"Don't worry, Mum," said Julian. "We won't forget anything."

But Pat had already forgotten something – his keys! When they got home they couldn't get in!

"**Meow!**" said Jess. He jumped in through a window.

Julian followed him and opened the door for Pat.

Julian made a peanut butter sandwich and put it in his lunch box.

"We're late," said Pat. "I'll drop you at school on my way to work."

When Pat got to the Post Office, he laughed. Mrs Goggins' dog, Bonnie, was sitting on the scales! "Are you going to post her?" asked Pat.

"No," said Mrs Goggins. "I'm weighing her. She's always hungry, but she's losing weight."

"That's not good," said Pat.

He took Mrs Goggins and Bonnie to see Amy, the vet.

"All her food was gone this morning," Mrs Goggins told Amy. "But she wanted more."

"Give her some more food when you get home," said Amy. "I'll call in later to see how she is."

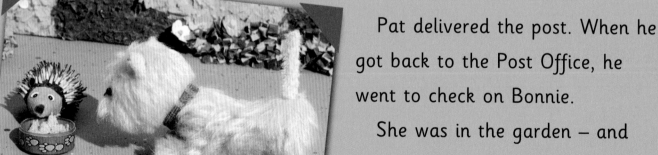

Pat delivered the post. When he got back to the Post Office, he went to check on Bonnie.

She was in the garden – and so was a hedgehog. It was eating her food!

"Woof, woof!" said Bonnie.

Woof, woof!

"So that's why she's always hungry!" said Mrs Goggins. "The hedgehog's been eating her food!"

The hedgehog scurried away.

"I'll catch it and take it into the countryside," said Pat. He put some of Bonnie's food into a cardboard box and propped it open with a stick.

After a while, the hedgehog went into the box and Pat pulled a string on the stick. It fell away and the flap closed.

"Got him!" said Pat.

"Got him!"

When Amy arrived, they took the hedgehog out into the countryside in her jeep.

That night, everything was quiet. The only sound that could be heard was **snuffle-snuffle-snuffle!** The hedgehog was going back to Greendale!

In the morning, Julian went to work with Pat. There was a surprise waiting for them. The hedgehog was back – with three babies!

"The he is a she!" said Pat. "The mummy hedgehog came back for her babies."

Snuffle-snuffle-snuffle!

Pat and Julian built a house to keep them safe.
The hedgehog family **sniffled** and **snuffled**, then they went inside.
"They like it!" said Julian.

"That's grand," said Mrs Goggins.
"The hedgehogs have a lovely
house and now Bonnie can eat
her food in peace."
"Woof!" said Bonnie.
"Meow!" said Jess.
Pat laughed. "Now Bonnie only
has to share it with Jess!"

Postman Pat's Noisy Day

Read this story with me. When you see a picture, say the name.
Don't forget to make the noises!

Pat   Jess   Julian   PC Selby   Sara

Jeff   Meera   Tom   Ted   Katy

 saw sweeping up leaves.

Swosh-swosh-swosh! went the broom.

 blew across the top of a bottle: **hoo-hoo-hoo!**

 blew his whistle: peep-peep-

peep! "What good sounds!" said  .

 worked with blocks of sandpaper:

ssh-ssh-ssh! "That's another great

sound!" said  .  banged

horseshoes together: clink-clink-clink!

The noises gave  an idea. "Meet

me at the school later,"  said to

 and his friends. "We're going to

make music!"

Later,  gave a tin of coffee

beans to shake: ratta-ratta-ratta!

 rubbed two blocks of sandpaper

together: **ssh-ssh-ssh!** and

blew a whistle: **peep-peep-peep!**

 played the horseshoes: **clink-**

clink-clink! "Making music is fun!" said

. Even joined in. **"Meow!"**

said .

"Meow-meow-meow!"

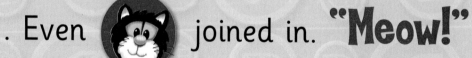

Making music was fun!

Can you answer these questions about the picture story?

1. What sound did Katy make?

2. What did Sara use to make a **clink-clink-clink!** sound?

3. Meera's tin went ratta-ratta-ratta! What was in the tin?

4. What sound did Pat make?

5. What sound did Tom make with a bottle?

ANSWERS: 1. Ssh-ssh-sshl; 2. Horseshoes; 3. Coffee beans; 4. Peep-peep-peep!; 5. Hoo-hoo-hoo!

Postman Pat the Hilltop Hero

One morning, Pat had a job to do before he went to work. He climbed a ladder to get rid of the leaves that were blocking the gutter on the roof.

"Thanks, Pat," said Sara. "I know you don't like heights."

Later on, Pat took some post to Thompson Ground.

Bill was helping his dad put some sheep into the trailer.

"We're moving them up to the hills near Greendale Crag," said Alf. "There's more grass for them there."

Bill patted his pet sheep, Bessie. "I wish Bessie could stay on the farm," he said.

Bessie agreed! "Baaaaaa!"

Baaaaaa!

Pat gave Bill a lift to the railway station where Julian, Meera and Sara were waiting. Ajay was taking them all on a walk to Greendale Crag.

Ajay followed his map. "This way," he said. "Through this gate and across the field."

Ajay closed the gate carefully, but it swung open again!

Alf had put his sheep in the next field. Bessie and another sheep ran out through the gate. They wanted to go back to the farm!

Pat was driving back to Greendale when he saw the sheep on the edge of the crag. "That's Bessie!" he said. "She shouldn't be up here!"

Pat tried to move the sheep away from the cliff. But Bessie was scared and she ran off down a steep path. She got stuck on a tiny ledge!

Ajay and the children were sitting around a camp fire at the bottom of the crag when Bill heard, "Baaaaaa!"

"That's Bessie!" he said.

Pat went to the edge of the cliff and shouted down. "Bessie's stuck!" he said. "Get help, Ajay!"

Baaaaaa!

Ajay found Amy in her jeep and told her about Bessie.

Amy drove to the top of the crag. She put on a harness and tied her climbing rope to a tree.

"Ready!" said Amy, and she swung out over the edge of the cliff.

Down she went,

down ...

down ...

down.

When she got to the ledge, Amy put a harness on Bessie.

"Baaa, baaa!" said Bessie. She was very pleased to see her.

But when Amy started to climb down, the rope got stuck on a rock. Amy and Bessie swayed around in mid-air!

"You'll have to climb down and free it, Pat!" said Amy.

Pat gulped. "Erm ... all right," he said. "Hold on, I'm coming!"

Pat put on a harness and tied a rope around the tree. Then he took a big, deep breath – and stepped over the edge of the cliff!

Down he went,

down ...

down ...

down.

Bill and the others watched from the bottom of the crag.

"Your dad's really brave, Julian," said Bill.

"I know," said Julian. "And he's scared of heights!"

Pat pulled Amy's rope free and she climbed down with Bessie. Bill was so pleased to see her that he gave her a big hug.

Bessie was pleased to see Bill, too. **"Baaa, baaa, baaa!"** she bleated.

When Pat climbed down, Julian gave him an extra big hug. "I thought you were afraid of heights, Dad," he said.

"I am," said Pat. "But I had to rescue Amy and Bessie, didn't I?"

Bill clapped and the others joined in. "Three cheers for Pat!" he said. "What a hero!"

Pat the Hero!

Pat was a real hero when he rescued Amy and Bessie. He climbed down the cliff, even though he doesn't like heights!

1

These pictures look the same, but there are 5 things that are different in picture 2. Can you spot the differences?

ANSWERS: 1. The bush on the cliff is missing; 2. Jess has appeared; 3. The bobble on Ajay's hat is missing; 4. A plate is missing; 5. Meera's boots are a different colour.

Postman Pat's Pet Rescue

When Julian came down for breakfast one morning, he sneezed:
"Atishoo! Atishoo!"

"You've got a cold," said Pat. "Stay at home today and I'll look after you. Mrs Goggins will deliver the post for me."

Pat took Julian back to bed.

"Can't I sit on the sofa and watch television?" asked Julian.

"No," said Pat. "Stay in bed. If you need anything, just ring this little bell and I'll come up."

Naughty Julian wasn't really very ill. He thought a day off school would be fun, but it wasn't! "Oh, this is so b-o-r-i-n-g," he said.

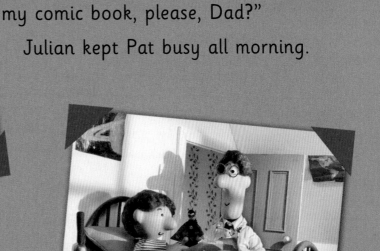

Ring! Julian rang the bell. When Pat came in he said, "Could you bring me my comic book, please, Dad?"

Julian kept Pat busy all morning.

Ring! "I need a drink," said Julian.

Ring! "Can I have my superhero toy?"

Ring! "Will you bring my truck?"

Pat and Julian didn't have any time for Jess, so Jess went off into the village. He met Bonnie there, and they ran off to an old well.

"Woof!" said Bonnie.

"Meow!" said Jess.

They ran round and round, faster and faster. But when Jess stopped and looked over the edge, he fell in!

"Meooooooow!" howled Jess. He was stuck, and his paw hurt.

Meoooooooow!

Woof!

Bonnie looked into the well.

"Woof!" she barked, and ran off to get help.

Bonnie found Mrs Goggins. "Woof!" she barked, but Mrs Goggins didn't know what she wanted.

So Bonnie ran off to find Amy. "Woof!" she barked, tugging at Amy's trousers. "Woof!"

Amy understood! "You want me to follow you!" she said.

"Woof!" barked Bonnie, and she led Amy to the well.

Amy used ropes to climb down inside. She put Jess in a rescue cage and climbed out with him. Then she took Jess to the animal clinic and x-rayed his paw. It was broken!

Later, Sara had just come home from work when Amy rang to tell her about Jess.

"He fell down a hole and broke his leg," Sara told Pat and Julian. "Amy's looking after him at the clinic."

"Dad, it's my fault," said Julian. "If you hadn't been looking after me, Jess wouldn't have gone off, and he'd be OK ..."

"You can't help being ill," said Pat.

"But I'm not really ill," said Julian. "I was a bit sniffly at first, but then I pretended."

"Hmm," said Pat. "I see."

Pat, Sara and Julian went to collect Jess.

"Thanks for looking after him, Amy," said Pat. **"Atishoo! Atishoo!"**

Pat had caught Julian's cold! When he got home it was his turn to stay in bed.

Ring, ring! Now it was Julian's turn to look after his dad!

Count with Postman Pat

Mrs Goggins sells all sorts of things in the Post Office shop!

Look at the big picture and count the numbers of things on the shelves.
Then circle a number.

a How many orange jars can you see?

1   2   3   4   5

b How many bottles of pop?

1   2   3   4   5

c How many packets of crackers?

1   2   3   4   5

d How many tins of cat food?

1   2   3   4   5

ANSWERS: a. 2, b. 3, c. 4, d. 5.

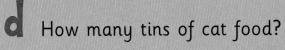

Postman Pat and the Go-kart Race

Mrs Goggins told everyone about the Greendale Go-kart Race. She explained the rules. "You must make your own go-kart. You can push, pull or pedal it. But you can't use an engine."

Pat, PC Selby, Ajay and Alf got busy making their karts. But things didn't go too well!

First, Pat's kart rattled, shook, then fell apart ...

Ooow!

PC Selby hit his thumb with a hammer ...

Ajay ended up head-first in his Greendale Rocket-kart ...

Argh!

And Alf's tractor-kart zoomed off down a hill!

Eeee!

PC Selby went to see Ted. "Can I borrow an electric engine?" he asked. "It's for ... er ... police business."

"All right," said Ted. "But remember, the engine won't ..." But PC Selby had gone.

Ajay borrowed an engine, and so did Alf. They didn't listen to Ted either.

Pat made a wind sail for his kart. "When the wind blows it goes really fast," he said. But the kart went **SO** fast that it crashed and ended up in pieces!

Later that day, Julian met up with Meera, Bill and Lucy.

"My dad's really bad at making go-karts," said Meera.

"So's mine," said Julian.

"Mine won't even let me help," said Bill.

"Let's make our own go-kart," said Lucy. "A kids'-kart."

"Yes!" said Julian. "We'll use what's left of Dad's kart. It's in bits, but it just needs ... um ... a bit of work."

On the day of the race all the go-karts lined up. Jeff said, "Everybody ready?"

"Ready!" said Ajay in his green Rocket-kart.
"Ready!" said Alf in his red tractor-kart.
"Ready!" said PC Selby in his blue police-car-kart.
"Ready!" said Julian in his pedal-kart.
"On your marks, get set ... go!" said Jeff.

Ajay, Alf and PC Selby switched on the engines of their karts and zoomed off.

Julian pedalled as fast as he could, but his kart was soon left behind.

"Does Julian's kart have an engine?" Ted asked Pat.

"Oh, no," said Pat. "That's against the rules. There are no engines allowed."

"Oh ..." said Ted.

The go-karts zoomed around the village.

First Alf was in the lead. Then Ajay. Then PC Selby.

Poor Julian was so slow that they all passed him on their second lap.

Minutes later Ajay, PC Selby and Alf sped past the finishing line. Jeff waved his flag, but they didn't stop.

"What's happening?" asked Pat.

"They wouldn't listen when I warned them about the engines," said Ted. "They switch **ON**, but they won't switch **OFF!**"

PC Selby, Alf and Ajay moved the **STOP** switch backwards and forwards, but the karts didn't stop. They sped out of the village on the road to Greendale Crag!

When Julian's pedal-kart got to the finishing line for the first time, Pat got in. He fitted the wind sail and they set off after the runaway karts.

The wind-kart sped along, and Pat and Julian watched as Ajay flew into a bush ...

Alf crashed into a bale of hay ...

and PC Selby landed in a pile of manure!

"**Urrgh!**" said Pat.

"What a pong!" said Julian.

Later on, Jeff announced the result of the race. "Alf, Ajay and PC Selby cheated by using engines," he said. "So the winners of the Greendale Go-kart Race are – Julian, Meera, Bill and Lucy!"

Everyone clapped and cheered:

"Hip, hip, hooray!"

"Hip, hip, hooray!"

The Greendale Go-kart Race Game

Now it's your turn to take part in the Greendale Go-kart Race! Play this game with a friend. You need:

- a die
- a counter each

Here's how to play.

1. Put your counters on the starting line.

2. Take turns to roll the die and move along the track. If you roll 2, move 2 spaces, and so on.

- If you land on a **red** flag, miss a turn.
- If you land on a **green** flag, have an extra turn.

The first player to cross the finishing line wins the race!

player **1**

player **2**

START

Postman Pat's Christmas Eve

It was Christmas Eve in Greendale, and the village was covered in a soft snowy blanket.

The Post Office was full of mail sacks.

"What a lot of post!" said Pat. "I hope I get it delivered in time! It's the Christmas show tonight and I don't want to miss it. Meera's Cinderella and Julian is Prince Charming!"

"Meow!" said Jess.

"Oh yes, I nearly forgot," said Pat. "Jess is Cinderella's cat and Pumpkin's going to pull the coach."

Pat took the post to the village hall. It was very noisy!

"It's the last rehearsal before the show," said Jeff.

"But everyone's being silly," said Meera.

Just then Bill swooped in on his skateboard. "Ugly sister coming through!" he said, and Jess leapt into the air and bumped into the scenery. "Meow!" said Jess.

"This is awful!" cried Meera. "No one's taking it seriously!"

63

Ajay had set off extra early to collect the village Christmas tree from Pencaster. But the snow was very thick, and the Rocket was still a long way from Greendale.

Ajay stopped at the Halt to fill the Rocket's boiler with water, but the water was frozen! "I hope we've got enough to get us home," he said.

When Pat had delivered all the post, he went to the station to help Ajay with the tree. But he still hadn't arrived, and Nisha was worried. "I'll find him," said Pat.

Out in the countryside, the Rocket was still chugging along ... until a snowdrift blocked the line.

"I've got some digging to do," said Ajay. But he had forgotten the shovel! The Rocket was stuck in the snow!

Pat drove up a steep lane, looking for Ajay. But the van's wheels spun in the snow. Then it skidded and stopped. "What do I do now?" said Pat.

Then he had an idea!

Pat steered the van backwards down the hill into the village.

"Can I borrow Pumpkin, Amy?" said Pat. "I need to find Ajay and the Rocket. Pumpkin can go where my van can't."

Just then, Ted arrived with the sleigh that was going to be Cinderella's coach.

"That's just what I need!" said Pat, and soon Pumpkin was trotting through the snow pulling Pat in the sleigh.

When Pat found Ajay, they put the tree on the sleigh and set off back to Greendale.

Clever Pumpkin knew the way, even in the snow!

"Well done, Meera!"

They got back in time to hear the audience cheering and clapping at the end of the show.

"Well done, Meera!" said Ajay. "Now come outside, everyone. There's a special surprise on the village green!"

It was the Christmas tree!

"**Wow!**" said Meera. "You and Pat even put presents under the tree, Dad!"

Just then, they heard the tinkle of sleigh bells and a jolly laugh. Pat smiled. "We didn't bring the presents," he said. "But I think I know who did! Do you? Merry Christmas, everyone!"

Pat's Quiz

Can you answer these questions? Look back through the book to find the answers.

1 Who has a car with the number plate DR 1?

2 What is the name of Amy's horse? Is it:
- **a.** Pollyanna
- **b.** Pumpkin or
- **c.** Petal?

3 In Postman Pat and the Greendale Knights, who fired a water hose at Ted?

4 Bill's pet sheep is called Bessie. True or false?

5 In **Postman Pat's Pet Rescue**, who fell down the well and broke his leg?

6 What is the name of the Greendale Light Railway engine?

Royal
E℞ Mail

G.R.

G.R.

7 In **Postman Pat and the Go-kart Race**, who raced in a red tractor-kart?

8 Where does Sara work? Is it:
a. Greendale Primary School or
b. Greendale Station café?

9 In **Postman Pat's Christmas Eve**, who played the part of Cinderella?

10 In **Postman Pat's Hedgehog Hideaway**, whose food did the hedgehog eat?

ANSWERS: 1. Doctor Gilbertson; 2. b. Pumpkin; 3. Lucy; 4. True; 5. Jess; 6. The Greendale Rocket; 7. Alf Thompson; 8. b. Greendale Station café; 9. Meera; 10. Bonnie's.

69